April Fool!

By Leland B. Jacobs

Drawings by Lou Cunette

GARRARD PUBLISHING COMPANY
CHAMPAIGN, ILLINOIS

April Fool!

Watch out!
It's April Fools' Day.
Will someone
play a trick on you?
Watch out!

Be very careful
that no one gives you:

a pocketbook
on a string

a candy
full of pepper

an apple
with a worm

or a buzzer
in your hand.

Watch out!

"Hi, there, Nancy,"
called her father.
"Have a good day."
"Thanks, dad," called Nancy.
"What's that bug
on your dress?" he asked.

"What bug?" Nancy yelled.
"APRIL FOOL!" said her father.

"Hi, there, Nancy,"
said the elephant.
"Let me give you
a present."
"Is it a ride
on your back?"
asked Nancy.

"No," said the elephant.
"It's a shower bath!
APRIL FOOL!"

"Hello, there, Nancy,"
said the brown bear.
"I have something
for you."
"Is it honey?"
asked Nancy.

"No," said the bear.
"It's a bear hug!
APRIL FOOL!"

"Good morning, Nancy,"
said Jimmy.
"Would you like
a piece of gum?"
"Yes," said Nancy.

"Ha-ha!
It's an empty paper,"
shouted Jimmy.
"APRIL FOOL!"

"Booooo! Nancy,"
said the ghost.
"I want
to give you something."
"Is it a scare?"
asked Nancy.

"Yes," cried the ghost.
"Whoooooooooo!
APRIL FOOL!"

"Hello, Nancy,"
said the blue jay.
"Let me give you
a nice treat."
"Is it
a pretty blue feather?"
asked Nancy.

"No," said the blue jay.
"It's a worm!
APRIL FOOL!"

"Good morning, Nancy,"
said the baker.
"I have a present
for you."
"Is it a cookie?"
Nancy asked.

"No," said the baker.
"A mud pie!
APRIL FOOL!"

"Nancy, my girl,"
said the pirate.
"Come and get
your present."
"Is it gold?"
Nancy asked.

"No," said the pirate.
"Play money!
APRIL FOOL!"

"Hello, Nancy,"
said the goat.
"I have something
for you."
"What is it?"
asked Nancy.

"Come over here,"
said the goat.
"APRIL FOOL!"

"Hi, there, Nancy,"
said Sally and Sue.
"We have a present
for you.
Open it now!"

"APRIL FOOL!"
shouted the girls.

"Hee-hee,"
said the witch.
"There's a treat
for you in my cave."
"Is it a black kitten?"
asked Nancy.

"No, it's not
a black kitten,"
said the witch.
"It's a bowl
of magic brew!
Hee-hee-hee!
APRIL FOOL!"

"Come in, Nancy,"
said the magician.
"I have a surprise
for you."
"Is it a rabbit
in a hat?" asked Nancy.

"Yes,"
said the magician.
"APRIL FOOL!"

"Hi, Nancy,"
said the fireman.
"Let me give you
something."
"What is it?"
asked Nancy.
"A fire hat?"

"No,"
said the fireman.
"A firefly!
APRIL FOOL!"

"Hi, there, Nancy,"
called the circus clown.
"I have something
for you."
"Is it a balloon?"
asked Nancy.

"No," said the clown.
"It's not a balloon.
It's a flower.
APRIL FOOL!"

"Good evening, Nancy,"
called the fisherman.
"Would you like
a present?"
"Yes," said Nancy.
"Is it a big fish?"

"No, it's not
a big fish,"
said the fisherman.
"It's a crab.
APRIL FOOL!"

"Hi, Nancy,"
shouted Tim and Tommy.
"We have a bag
for you."
"Is it a bag
of popcorn?"
asked Nancy.

"No," said the boys.
"It's not popcorn.
APRIL FOOL!"

"Hello, Nancy,"
said mother.
"Dinner is ready."
"Will I like dinner?"
asked Nancy.

"Yes," said mother,
"if you like
chocolate chicken,
blue milk,
and pickle ice cream!"

"Mother and dad,
come here," yelled Nancy.
"There is a spider
in my bed!"
"Where? Where?"
asked her mother
and father.

"APRIL FOOL!"
shouted Nancy.